A Dragon of Inn

Written & Illustrated by Daria Chernysheva
Text and illustrations copyright © 2012 by B'nai B'rith International

ISBN: 978-0-578-10606-9

Published as part of the *Diverse Minds Youth Writing Challenge* by:

B'NAI B'RITH INTERNATIONAL

2020 K Street NW, 7th Floor
Washington, DC 20006
202-857-6600
www.bnaibrith.org

A Dragon
of Inn

Written & Illustrated by
Daria Chernysheva

In the middle of blue waters, there lay the Isle of Inn.

It was a beautiful land, a place full of farmers and miners, painters and musicians – who all happened to be dragons.

The Sun-Dragons lived in the east, where they tended golden fields full of wheat and rye. They flew with their wings outstretched beneath the warm golden sun.

The Moon-Dragons lived in the west, and they were great miners. They dug deep into the mountains and brought gems out of the earth. They made scepters of sapphires and crowns of rubies and flew, glittering, beneath the silver moon.

The Wind-Dragons lived in the north, in stone castles built very long ago. There they mixed colors of all shades, and spent their days painting landscapes and portraits of Dragon Royalty.

The Water-Dragons of the south lived by the warm waters of the sea and played music. They were very skilled with flutes and cellos, although of course they knew how to play every instrument ever invented.

How beautiful, how rich was the Isle of Inn! But in the land there was also a great sadness. None of the dragons spoke to each other. They did not trade their goods. The Sun-Dragons did not get to see the beautiful paintings, and the Wind-Dragons did not eat delicious bread. The Water-Dragons had never seen a gemstone and the Moon-Dragons had never heard the tune of a violin.

It was all because of a quarrel long, long ago. The great-great-great-great-great grandfathers of the dragon tribes, whose names no one remembered, had become angry at each other. No one knew why. And ever since then, the dragon tribes lived separately. They did not visit each other. They did not write letters. Each tribe pretended like the others did not exist.

But in this rich land full of sadness, there was also hope.

Right in the middle of the island lay the Forest of In-Between. In that forest lived no dragons - save one.

His name was Hallie.

Hallie lived all alone. He did not
belong to any of the dragon tribes,
because he could not choose just one.

He wanted to be a Moon-Dragon
because he enjoyed examining
gemstones.

He wanted to be a Sun-Dragon,
because he loved baking pastries.

He wanted to be a
Wind-Dragon because
he had always wanted
to paint a still-life.

And he wanted to be a Water-Dragon
because he could play the cello really,
really well.

Hallie knew he could be happy only if he did all these things together. But he also knew that the dragon tribes were still angry over their great-great-great-great-great grandfathers' quarrel and would not approve.

So Hallie spent his days lying beneath the green leaves, dreaming of pastries and painting, of mines and music.

All was quiet, all seemed well. Until one day...

Great blue clouds rolled in from the sea and covered the sky. The waves at the shore became angry and jumped high, almost reaching the cliffs. The wind began to blow through the branches of the Forest of In-Between. Over the fields, over the mountains, over the castles, over the beaches, a rain began to fall. The Great Storm had come.

The dragons knew about the Great Storm, but the last one had happened very long ago, even before the great-great-great-great-great grandfathers' quarrel. The dragons did not know how to shelter themselves from the wind and the rain.

"We will be all right, we have the food we need," said the Sun-Dragons, but the rain fell too heavily on the golden fields.

"We have our tunnels to hide in," said the Moon-Dragons, but the tunnels were windy, lonely and cold.

"We can paint to pass the time," said the Wind-Dragons, but food supplies in the castles were low.

"We have our music to keep our spirits up," said the Water-Dragons, but the rain leaked through the roofs and damaged the instruments.

The dragons might have continued to be their stubborn selves and may have never gotten to shelter, if it weren't for Hallie, the little dragon from the Forest of In-Between.

Hallie flew as quickly as he could to the Moon-Dragons, who knew the way of the tunnels and caves.

"Moon-Dragons, you must let everybody into your caves!" cried Hallie. "You must let the Sun-Dragons, the Wind-Dragons and the Water-Dragons shelter together!"

The Moon-Dragons could not believe their ears. "Shelter with the other tribes?" they asked. "But we do not speak to the other tribes! We do not work together!"

"But you must," said Hallie.

The he flew to the Sun-Dragons.
"Sun-Dragons, take your bags of flour
and corn with you and fly to the
Moon-Dragons! Take shelter with the
other tribes in the mountains!"

The Sun-Dragons looked at each other.
"But this is impossible! We do not work
with other dragons!"

"But you must," said Hallie.

Then Hallie flew to the Wind-Dragons. "Wind-Dragons, take your paints and brushes, and make your way to the shelter with the other dragons in the mountains!"

The Wind-Dragons laughed. "We will not go to the mountains! We do not work with the other dragons!"

"But you must," said Hallie.

Then Hallie flew at last down to the Water-Dragons and cried, "Water-Dragons, take your cellos, flutes and violins. Fly to the mountains to take shelter with the other dragon tribes!"

And the Water-Dragons shook their heads, clutching their soaked instruments. "No, we cannot do that. We cannot work with other dragons."

"But you must!" said Hallie.

By that time the Great Storm had become very bad. The golden fields were flooded, the southern beaches were flooded and the water had even reached the castles in the north. At last the dragons realized they could not face the Great Storm alone.

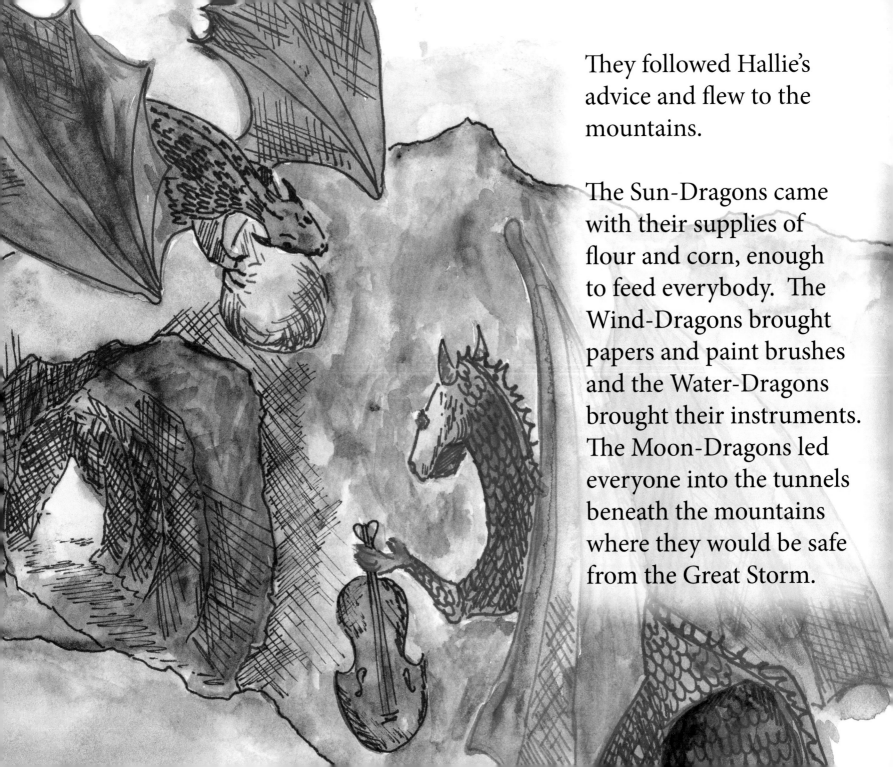

They followed Hallie's advice and flew to the mountains.

The Sun-Dragons came with their supplies of flour and corn, enough to feed everybody. The Wind-Dragons brought papers and paint brushes and the Water-Dragons brought their instruments. The Moon-Dragons led everyone into the tunnels beneath the mountains where they would be safe from the Great Storm.

The Great Storm raged for seven days. The rain fell, the earth shook and the winds howled. But in the tunnels of the Moon-Dragons, everybody was very cozy and very happy.

The Sun-Dragons baked bread and made enough pastries to feed everyone for the whole week. The Wind-Dragons painted warm pictures of sunshine and green trees to chase away all the gloom. The Water-Dragons played their instruments to keep everyone's spirits up.

And Hallie looked at all the dragon tribes and felt proud seeing everyone work together.

After seven days, the rains stopped and the clouds parted. The dragons came out of the tunnels to greet the sunshine. The Sun-Dragons came out, the Moon-Dragons came out, the Wind-Dragons came out and the Water-Dragons came out – but they did not separate themselves as before.

They knew each other as friends.

All the dragons looked around their island and they were very happy to have it back. Then they looked at Hallie.

"Hallie," said the dragons, "You were right. We were foolish to think that we could brave the Great Storm alone."

Hallie smiled. "It took all of you working together," he said. "It took the Moon-Dragons' knowledge of the mountains, the Sun-Dragons' crops, the Wind-Dragons' painting and the Water-Dragons' music to get everyone through this. Alone, your gifts were only so powerful. Together, they were mighty."

And then the dragons cheered little Hallie and set out for their homes. Except that this time, there were no borders. Sun, Mood, Wind and Water flew whatever which way! The dragons scattered to the north, south, east and west, flying not with their old tribes or their names, but with their new friends.

As the dragons resumed their lives on the Isle of Inn, everyone chose to do everything at once. Dragons who mined diamonds also found that they were very good at playing the flute. Dragons who baked pastries also painted landscapes of the new places they visited. And so the sadness in the land was chased away and the Isle of Inn became prosperous once more.

And as for Hallie? Oh, he managed to visit many different places and do many different things. He still lived in his forest from time to time. But now he was very happy. He did not have to choose between which gift to have, or what tribe to belong to; now, he could simply be a **Dragon of Inn**.

A Dragon of Inn, written & illustrated by Daria Chernysheva, was created as part of the B'nai B'rith International *Diverse Minds Youth Writing Challenge* in New York City.

The *Diverse Minds Youth Writing Challenge* is an education and awareness initiative created by B'nai B'rith International as part of its series of programs developed to combat bigotry through the promotion of tolerance and equality. The contest aims to present positive views about diversity to a broad range of youth in order to achieve tolerance within our communities.

Executed through public and private high schools within New York City, the contest asks high school students to write and illustrate a children's book that tells a story of diversity and tolerance. Participants are required to think about how these principles can improve our world, and then create innovative ways to teach these ideas to children through the creation of a book.

Book submissions were reviewed by a local judging panel comprised of business leaders, educators, arts administrators and community officials. Scholarship prizes in the amounts of $5,000, $2,000 and $1,000 are awarded to the first, second and third place winners, and the first-place winning book is professionally published and distributed to elementary schools, libraries and youth organizations within New York.

For more information about the program and next year's contests, please visit www.bnaibrith.org/diverseminds.

A Dragon of Inn

Written & Illustrated by
Daria Chernysheva

Brooklyn Technical High School
Brooklyn, NY

Teacher: Mr. Timothy Ree

Daria Chernysheva, a student at Brooklyn Technical High School, was selected as the first place winner of the 2012 *Diverse Minds Youth Writing Challenge*.

Daria spent most of her childhood reading fairytales and drawing caterpillars. In time — maybe after studying literature and languages — she hopes to write, write and write some more, particularly children's fantasy books.

SECOND PLACE WINNER

Color Coded

Written by
Yashoda Persaud

Illustrated by
Angela Chen

THIRD PLACE WINNER

Unmasked

Written & Illustrated by
Iris Dai

New York City Judging Panel

B'nai B'rith International would like to thank the following judging panel members for donating their time and talents to reviewing the finalists' submissions and selecting the winners for the 2012 *Diverse Minds Youth Writing Challenge.*

Robin Adelson
Executive Director
Children's Book Council

Alexander Baumgarten
Director of Government Relations
The Episcopal Church, Washington

Lawrence Leibowitz
Chief Operating Officer
NYSE Euronext

Hannie Chia
Education Programs Manager
The Bronx Museum of the Arts

Ahmad Corbitt
Director of Public and International Affairs
The Church of Jesus Christ of Latter-day Saints

Toby Graff
Senior Vice President, Public Affairs
USA Network

Raymond W. Kelly
Commissioner
New York City Police Department

Naomi Kleinberg
Editorial Director, Sesame Street Publishing Program
Random House Children's Books

Lawrence J. Krule
President
Jewish Book Council

Sunny Larson
Director of Public Outreach
The Fund for Public Schools

Andrea Louie
Executive Director
Asian American Arts Alliance

Rhonda Love
Program Director
B'nai B'rith International

Daniel S. Mariaschin
Executive Vice President
B'nai B'rith International

Dr. Anthony W. Marx
President & CEO
The New York Public Library

Stephen Mooser
President
Society of Children's Book Writers & Illustrators

Adam Rudich
Director of Operations & Community Affairs
Museum of Tolerance New York

Amy Ruggerio
Director of Education & Model UN
United Nations Foundation

B'NAI B'RITH INTERNATIONAL

B'nai B'rith International is the most widely known Jewish humanitarian, human rights, and advocacy organization. Since 1843, B'nai B'rith has been dedicated to improving the quality of life for those throughout the country and around the globe through programs that promote its commitment to youth, health education, senior housing, community service, public action and disaster relief. B'nai B'rith International's reach extends to more than 50 countries around the world.

Today, B'nai B'rith International is a national and global leader in helping communities in crisis; providing senior housing and advocacy on issues of vital concern to seniors and their families; and promoting diversity and tolerance education to our nation's youth.

The work of B'nai B'rith International is focused in its Centers: Senior Services, Community Action, and Human Rights & Public Policy. These Centers provide the framework for intensive study of issues and thoughtful responses through the combined efforts of dedicated volunteer leaders and professional staff.

Allan J. Jacobs
International President

Daniel S. Mariachin
Executive Vice President

B'nai B'rith International • 2020 K Street, NW, 7th Floor • Washington, DC 20006
888-838-2499 • www.bnaibrith.org

Program Sponsor

NYSE Euronext

F O U N D A T I O N .sm

B'nai B'rith International would like to thank the NYSE Euronext Foundation for their continued support of the *Diverse Minds Youth Writing Challenge* in New York City. Their generous grant provided the funds necessary for B'nai B'rith to publish **A Dragon of Inn** and donate a copy of it to each library and elementary school in New York City.

The NYSE Euronext Foundation is a private philanthropic foundation established by the New York Stock Exchange in 1983. It directs its philanthropic resources to innovative and effective organizations, programs, and projects that meet community needs within its priority areas of funding: Financial Literacy Education, Developing Economic Opportunity, and Entrepreneurship. It seeks to address the needs of communities in all areas of the globe where NYSE Euronext maintains a business presence and funds both new and proven charitable endeavors that confer a broad public benefit.

Daniel S. Mariaschin, Executive Vice President of B'nai B'rith, joins the first, second and third place winners of the New York City Challenge. The New York Stock Exchange generously hosts the Award Presentation Event each year.

Students compete in The Stock Market Game, an on-line educational program sponsored by SIFMA Foundation. The NYSE Euronext Foundation has been a supporter of The Stock Market Game since 1984.

Program Sponsor

CHARACTERS UNITE

characters welcome. **USA**

B'nai B'rith International would like to thank USA Network and the Characters Unite campaign for their support of the *Diverse Minds Youth Writing Challenge* in New York City.

USA Network's Characters Unite initiative is dedicated to promoting diversity, tolerance and acceptance, themes B'nai B'rith aims to relay to youth through its writing challenge. Characters Unite includes original programming and PSAs, digital content and community and school events across the country to help combat prejudice, hate and discrimination.

The #1 network in all of basic cable, USA Network is seen in 115 million U.S. homes. A division of NBCUniversal, USA is a leader in scripted programming with a powerful stable of originals and is home to spectacular live television with WWE MONDAY NIGHT RAW, blockbuster theatrical films and a broad portfolio of acquired series and entertainment events. The award-winning website is located at www.usanetwork.com. Characters Welcome.